SIR CUMFERENCE

GETS DECIMA'S POINT

DECIMALS

Cindy Neuschwander

ILLUSTRATED BY
Wayne Geehan

Charlesbridge

In memory of Helen, who was always fabulous—C. N.

With love to my two new grandchildren, Alden Carlson Geehan and Sloane Elizabeth Brenckle, and their parents Jonathan and Caroline Geehan and Mark and Amy Brenckle—W. G.

Published by Charlesbridge
9 Galen Street, Watertown, MA 02472
(617) 926-0329
www.charlesbridge.com

Printed in China
(hc) 10 9 8 7 6 5 4 3 2 1
(sc) 10 9 8 7 6 5 4 3 2 1

Library of Congress Cataloging-in-Publication Data
Names: Neuschwander, Cindy, author. | Geehan, Wayne, illustrator.
Title: Sir Cumference Gets Decima's Point / Cindy Neuschwander; illustrated by Wayne Geehan.
Description: Watertown, MA: Charlesbridge, [2020]
Identifiers: LCCN 2019016448 (print) | LCCN 2019018071 (ebook) | ISBN 9781632895875 (e-book) | ISBN 9781570917646 (hardcover) | ISBN 9781570918452 (paperback)
Subjects: LCSH: Decimal fractions—Juvenile literature. | Counting—Juvenile literature.
Classification: LCC QA242 (ebook) | LCC QA242 .N475 2020 (print) | DDC 513.2/65—dc23
LC record available at https://lccn.loc.gov/2019016448

Illustrations done in acrylic paint on canvas
Display type set in Realist by Graptail
Text type set in Adobe Garamond Pro by Adobe Systems
Color separations by Colourscan Print Co Pte Ltd, Singapore
Printed by 1010 Printing International Limited in Huizhou, Guangdong, China
Production supervision by Brian G. Walker
Designed by Martha MacLeod Sikkema

"It's nearly sunrise," said Bart Graf, the baker, stoking the oven.

His business partner, Pia of Chartre, yawned. "Let's bake Crème de la Crumb toda—"

Creeeak . . . CRASH! Before Pia could finish her sentence, a large, hairy beast wrenched open the bakery door, stepped inside, and grabbed her.

"I am Tenntt the Ogre," boomed the creature, "and I am borrowing this baker."

Together they disappeared into the weak light of dawn.

Bart was greatly shaken. He sprinted up to the castle and informed Sir Cumference and Lady Di.

"Pia? Gone? Where?" asked Sir Cumference incredulously.

"We must search for her immediately!" exclaimed Lady Di.

"I might have an idea how to find her," Bart said. "We'll follow the trail of fluff from the ogre's tunic."

Meanwhile, Pia stood inside a manor house deep in the backcountry. Twelve huge ogres surrounded her.

"What do you want?" she asked.

The smallest ogre replied, "I'm Decima. These are my parents, Tenntt and Hoondrit, and my nine older sisters. Tonight we're celebrating our 100th Jubilee as the gatekeepers of the bridge over the River Tens. We're preparing a feast, but we need help!"

Pia relaxed. "Cooking I can do," she said. "Point me to the kitchen."

The place was in shambles. After tidying up, Pia assigned jobs to the ogres. "Decima, you and I will make the dessert."

Soon the kitchen was a sizzling, simmering cloud of delicious aromas. Pia and Decima mixed ten batches of Crème de la Crumb and poured them into immense square baking pans.

When the first pans were cooling on the windowsill, Decima's oldest sister gobbled one down entirely. "Heavenly!" she declared.

"Una!" cried Decima. "You ate one whole batch!"

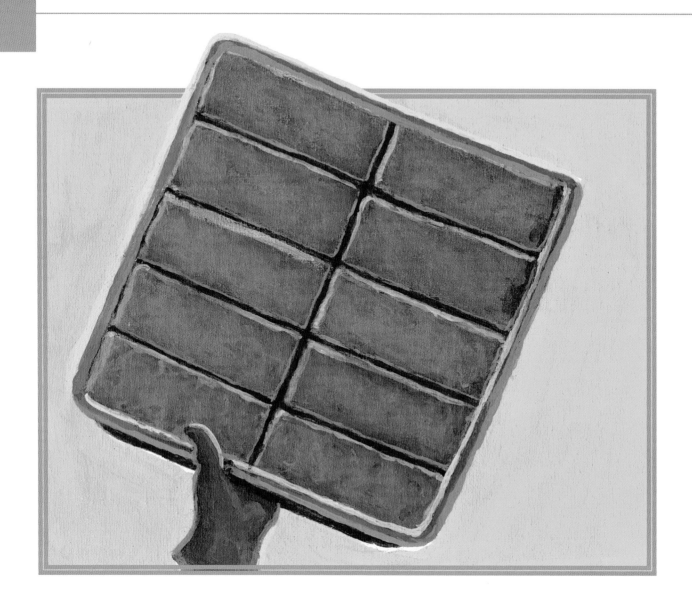

Tenntt was close behind. "Such an ambrosial smell! May we share another?"

"Here, Father." Decima cut a second batch into ten equal portions. "I've named this size piece a Tenntt, after you."

"Thank you, my little sugarplum!" he said.

Decima gave the pieces to her two parents and eight other sisters.

After Hoondrit had eaten her slice, she said, "Oh, Decima! This is toothsome! Could we have some more to nibble on while we mash and mix our meal?"

Decima took a third tin and cut it into ten Tenntt-sized pieces. She cut each of these ten pieces into ten smaller, equal squares.

"Here are 100 Hoondrit-sized morsels, named for you," she said, hugging her mother.

"What a thoughtful daughter!" exclaimed Hoondrit.

Decima and Pia baked more dessert to replace what the ogres had eaten. Soon they had ten pans of delicious Créme de la Crumb.

"Pssst! Pia!" came a low voice from outside the kitchen window.

Surprised, Pia and the ogres looked up from their work.

"Intruders!" bellowed Tenntt, rushing toward them.

"These are my friends!" called Pia. "Let's ask them to lend a hand."

"Enter!" he roared joyfully.

So Sir Cumference, Lady Di, and Bart, reassured that Pia was unharmed, climbed in and got to work.

By late afternoon, all was ready. The ogre family changed into formal wear and joined their guests for the meal, while Pia and her team readied the desserts.

"How much on each plate?" asked Lady Di.

"I'm using Decima's system, slicing each whole pan into Tenntt-sized pieces," answered Pia.

Lady Di looked confused.

"Tenntts are ten equal parts in a whole pan," the baker explained.

WHUMP! Decima burst through the kitchen door. "Everyone wants dessert. . . . We need 85 pieces. NOW!"

"Dilly-icious, dilly-icious!" raved the ogres, drumming their spoons on the dining tables.

"Good thing we have ten batches," said Lady Di. "That's 100 servings."

Decima looked worried. "We should have more pieces on hand for eager eaters."

"Then I shall cut one pan into Hoondrits," Pia decided.

"Better hurry," answered Sir Cumference. "They're going *ogre* the top."

"Will this be enough?" Lady Di asked.

"Nine pans of Tenntts is nine times ten, or 90 pieces," figured Bart.

"Plus the 100 smaller slices in the Hoondrits pan," piped up Lady Di.

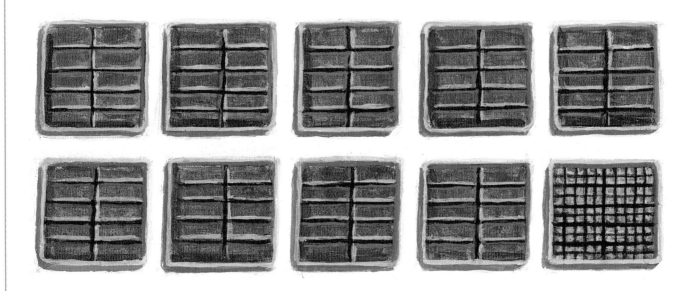

"That's 190 portions," said Pia happily. "With 85 ogres to serve, there's more than enough for everyone to have a bigger first piece and a smaller second helping."

Bart peered out through the kitchen doors. "Uh-oh! Uninvited guests have just landed in the rafters!" he announced.

Decima peeked out, too. "It's Tousander and his passel of 999 pesky pixies. They're sure to want dessert as well."

"We won't have enough unless the pixie helpings are smaller than Hoondrits," Decima reasoned. She took the Hoondrits pan and began to slice each of those 100 pieces into ten very tiny but equal slivers. "Little Tousander-sized bits," she said, smiling.

"A thousand servings from one pan? That's hardly more than crumbs," said Pia.

Decima shrugged. "Pixies are very small."

Frenzied fists started pounding on the dining room side of the sturdy kitchen doors.

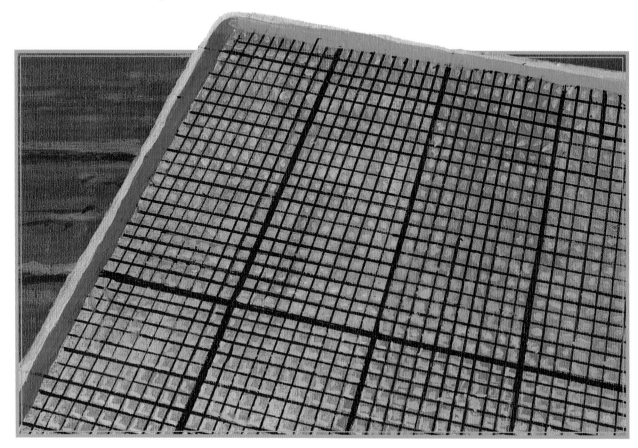

Ignoring the ogres' antics, Lady Di said, "I'm seeing a pattern to Decima's system. Every time we cut this dessert, we make it into pieces that are ten times smaller. A Tenntt is ten times smaller than one whole."

Bart nodded. "A Hoondrit is ten times smaller than one Tenntt."

"And a Tousander is ten times smaller than a Hoondrit!" exclaimed Sir Cumference.

C-R-A-A-A-C-K!
The door exploded into splinters, and a wave of ogres
flooded the kitchen while the pixies cheered from the rafters.

In the melee, a good deal of Crème de la Crumb was flung across the room. Stunned, the ogres began to cry. Sweet treats were so important.

Decima scolded them. "See what you've done! Go sit in the dining room. We'll count what's left and share it among you."

The ogres dried their tears and tried to wait patiently. Pia and her crew placed the remaining dessert on the head table.

"All right," said Decima, slipping on a clean apron. "I'll begin the count."

"And I'll record it for you," offered Bart.

"We have one whole pan of Tenntt-sized servings," announced Decima, "and one more Tenntt-sized piece in this next pan."

The quill pen worked poorly, so Bart wrote only enough to record the counts accurately. For *pan*, he used a tiny letter p. To the left of the p he wrote the number of whole pans and to the right, the number of pieces.

1p1

"Just five Tenntts in this one," counted Decima.
Bart wrote:

$$_p5$$

Decima continued. "And two Tenntts in this pan."
Bart wrote down:

$$_p2$$

Decima said, "That's it. There's no more."
The ogres held their breath as Bart added up what he had recorded.

$$1_p1 + {}_p5 + {}_p2 = 1_p8$$

"For the ogre guests," he announced, "there is one full pan of Tenntts and eight other Tenntt-sized slices."
"That's 18 pieces—not nearly enough!" one ogre cried as the rest of the guests moaned.

But Decima had an idea. "What if we cut them all into Hoondrits?"

Bart said, "That would be ten times more than the Tenntts, so I'd add them as Hoondrits instead."

He scribbled down:

$$1p10 + p50 + p20 = 1p80$$

"We'd have one whole pan of Hoondrits plus another 80 Hoondrits. That's 180 small portions. That's enough for each ogre to have at least two small pieces."

The ogres thumped their spoons approvingly on the tables as Decima began to slice Tenntts into Hoondrits.

"But what about the pixies?" Lady Di asked.

"Egads! We almost forgot their pan," said Sir Cumference. "Sadly, one piece of the thousand is missing."

Bart took the parchment and recorded

ₚ999

Lady Di announced, "There are 999 Tousander-sized slivers."

Faint, buzzy crying could be heard as the wee folk realized one of them would get no dessert.

"I'll give up my serving," said Tousander.

"For your noble gesture," responded Decima, "have a leftover Hoondrit piece."

There had never been a finer Jubilee celebration dessert.

As they left, Pia and her cooking crew received a rousing toast.

"To Pia and sweet treats!" cheered the ogres, hoisting their empty plates into the air.

"Many thanks!" she responded. "Come round to the bakery for a visit and some more Crème de la Crumb!"

The ogres beat a frequent path to Pia and Bart's bakery. The ogres and the townsfolk kept the two bakers very busy making Crème de la Crumb.

They wrote down their orders using Bart's handy abbreviations. After a while, all of Angleland was using Decima's system. Bart's tiny letter p soon looked more like a dot or a comma. It was called Decima's point.

Today, people all around the world use Decima's system— what we call the decimal system—for wholes and parts. Whole numbers are written first. A dot or a comma (mathematically known as a radix point) separates them from fractional numbers.

The place values recorded to the right of the dot or comma are known as tenths (Tenntt-sized pieces), hundredths (Hoondrit-sized pieces), and thousandths (Tousander-sized pieces). But these are just the first three of the fractional number places that can be written. Just as there are infinite whole number places, there are also infinite fractional number places.

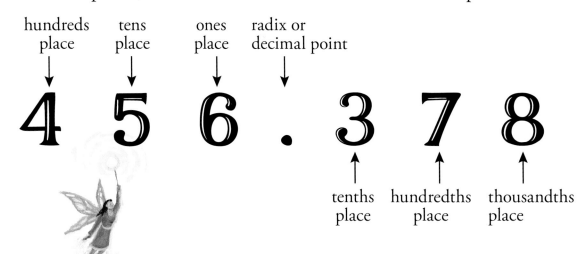

hundreds place   tens place   ones place   radix or decimal point

4 5 6 . 3 7 8

tenths place   hundredths place   thousandths place